PIPER MORGAN
JOINS THE CIRCUS

DON'T MISS PIPER'S OTHER ADVENTURES!

Piper Morgan in Charge!

COMING SOON:

Piper Morgan to the Rescue

ALSO BY STEPHANIE FARIS:

30 Days of No Gossip

25 Roses

PIPER MORGAN

JOINS THE CIRCUS

BY STEPHANIE FARIS

ILLUSTRATED BY LUCY FLEMING

♡

ALADDIN

New York   London   Toronto   Sydney   New Delhi

ALADDIN

An imprint of Simon & Schuster Children's Publishing Division

1230 Avenue of the Americas, New York, New York 10020

First Aladdin paperback edition August 2016

Text copyright © 2016 by Stephanie Faris

Illustrations copyright © 2016 by Lucy Fleming

Also available in an Aladdin hardcover edition.

All rights reserved, including the right of reproduction in whole or in part in any form.

ALADDIN is a trademark of Simon & Schuster, Inc., and related logo is a registered trademark of Simon & Schuster, Inc.

For information about special discounts for bulk purchases, please contact Simon & Schuster Special Sales at 1-866-506-1949 or business@simonandschuster.com.

The Simon & Schuster Speakers Bureau can bring authors to your live event. For more information or to book an event contact the Simon & Schuster Speakers Bureau at 1-866-248-3049 or visit our website at www.simonspeakers.com.

Book designed by Laura Lyn DiSiena

The text of this book was set New Baskerville.

Manufactured in the United States of America 0716 OFF

2 4 6 8 10 9 7 5 3 1

Library of Congress Control Number 2016932221

ISBN 978-1-4814-5709-5 (hc)

ISBN 9781-4814-5708-8 (pbk)

ISBN 9781-4814-5710-1 (eBook)

For Cambryn Nicole, who has grown into
a beautiful young woman

CHAPTER

★ 1 ★

Whoosh!

I stopped behind my mom, staring up at the big bus in front of me, my mouth hanging open. On the side of the bus was a big sign that read BIG TOP CIRCUS. Plus, there were pictures of elephants and tigers. Best of all, there were three others just like it, all lined up.

Just a little while ago I'd been upset that we were leaving my friends and my teachers and my school. But now I wasn't even thinking about that. I was thinking about how awesome it was that we were about to get on a big bus and go to the circus, where my mom would be working.

Buses were super noisy. *Whooshes* and hums and even honks as one bus drove by, its driver waving at ours. But that bus didn't have the words BIG TOP CIRCUS in huge letters on the side. Ours did.

"Keep up, Piper," Mom said, reaching out to take my hand. I had my new hot pink purse in that hand, so I switched it to the other and slipped my hand into my mom's much bigger one.

She was walking fast, which meant I had to run really, really hard to keep up. Lots of steps for every one Mom took. If I didn't keep up, I'd miss the bus and have to stay here.

I ran faster. I wanted to stay here, but even more I wanted to ride on the bus with animals on the side.

My mom's new job was as an assistant. That means she takes care of stuff for people. A person will send her jobs to take care of stuff for people, but the jobs are only temporary. "Temporary" is when something doesn't last long. Her last job lasted two days. The person said if my mom was willing to go anywhere, she might be able to find a job that would last a long time. As long as she wasn't fired again like she was from her last job. For now, we were going to live with the traveling circus people.

The bus made a loud *whoosh* noise just as we were stepping on. I thought we'd just made it and almost started jumping up and down. But when I turned around, there were still bunches of people standing outside. Bunches of suitcases, too. The bus wasn't leaving yet, just making funny noises.

"Let's find our seats," Mom said, tugging on my hand. I followed her, expecting to see ballerinas and stuff. Instead, there were just normal people, standing in the aisles and sitting in their seats.

Some guy was showing people where to go. He wasn't dressed up either. Just a boring old shirt and a boring old pair of pants. He looked like someone I'd see in the grocery store.

"Julie Morgan," Mom told him. "This is my daughter, Piper."

"Hi, Piper," the man said, leaning over to look at me and talking to me way too loud. Like I was four or something.

I didn't say anything, just looked at my mom. I gave her my "this guy is scaring me" look because . . . well . . . he was. But the good thing was, he stood back up and stopped talking to me.

"You're in the very back," the man told Mom in a very businessy tone. I noticed he didn't talk to *her* like she was four.

We went to our seats. There was a girl sitting in the seat in front of us, next to an older woman. She was about my age. She stood up in her seat and turned to stare down at me. That was all she did. Just stared.

"My name's Lexie, and this is my mom," she finally said, pointing to the person next to her. "What's your name?"

"Piper," I said. "Piper Morgan."

Her mom yelled at her to sit down, so

she disappeared. I thought for a second, then kneeled in my seat so I could talk to her. I could just see over the top of the seat.

"My mom said there are ballerinas in the circus," I told her.

She squirmed around in her seat and looked up at me. "There are not," she said.

I looked at my mom. She'd said so! But Mom was looking down at her phone. I decided to let it drop and ask Lexie if she wanted to be my new best friend.

"We just came from Florida," Lexie announced. "We had a circus on the beach."

"Awesome!" I said. I wondered where we were going now. Mom hadn't told me. It didn't matter. I was just glad I had a new friend.

"Do you want to be friends?" I asked.

I picked my best friend Dania out the

first day of kindergarten and we were friends for a very, very long time. Until we had to move.

"No," Lexie said. "I don't want friends."

She turned around and started playing some game. I was trying to think of something else to say, like, *Fine! I don't want to be your friend either*. But Mom made me sit down because the bus was going soon.

I would have pouted, but when I started to sit down, the best thing ever happened.

I saw a real-life ballerina!

FAIRGROUND FACT #1

Ringling Bros. and Barnum & Bailey Circus uses circus trains to get to your city. The trains have beds for the performers and workers and special cars for the animals. People line up by the tracks to see all the colorful train cars when they know the train is passing by.

Other circuses use RVs and buses to move from one place to the next. The people sleep in RVs, and the animals get to see the country on the interstate from the trucks and trailers. It's easier because they can get the animals and people to cities and towns that don't have railroad tracks.

Still, I think sleeping in a train car would be more fun, though. Don't you?

CHAPTER
★ 2 ★

Lexie was wrong. There *were* ballerinas.

The ballerina I saw was beautiful. She was tall, wearing a pink T-shirt and pink pants and no makeup. She had to be a ballerina. She even had her hair in a bun like ballerinas do.

"I have to go talk to Mr. Winkles," Mom said. "He's my new boss. But Miss Sarah will sit with you." She pointed to the lady in the pink outfit.

Miss Sarah gave me a big smile.

"This is Miss Sarah," Mom said. "She's a performer. I'll be right up here if you need me."

Mom walked away, leaving me with Miss Sarah. I wanted to know what a "performer" was and if it was like being a ballerina, but she was a new person. And new people make me shy.

"It's nice to meet you, Piper," Miss Sarah said. "How old are you?"

Grown-ups always ask that. Along with, "What grade are you in?" and "Do you have a best friend?" I always answer, but it's kind of annoying answering the same questions over and over and over.

"Seven," I answered.

"Seven," she repeated. "That's really big."

Not really, I thought, but I didn't say so.

"How old are you?" I asked.

She laughed. I wasn't sure why. She'd asked me, so why not?

"I'm nineteen," she said. "I'm one of the youngest performers. I help watch children like you while your parents work. Doesn't that sound like fun?"

I felt less shy now. "What do you do in the show?" I asked.

"I'm out in the audience during the show entertaining the crowds during the acts," she explained. "It's really fun. I usually do a dance before the tigers come into the ring."

I sat up straighter in my seat. She *was* like a ballerina. I'd met a true-life ballerina.

"Can you show me how to be a show performer?" I asked.

"I think I can do that," Miss Sarah said with a big smile.

I jumped out of my seat and looked down at "I don't want friends" Lexie. "Guess what?" I asked.

She looked up at me.

"I get to learn how to be a circus performer," I declared. "And you don't."

"Sit down, young lady," Lexie's mom scolded. It looked like the bus would be pulling away soon, so I sat down.

Lexie turned in her seat and said so that only I could hear, "Um, I'm *already* a performer. *I've* been with the circus for forever. Your mom's just filling in until Mr. Winkles's secretary gets back. Then you'll be gone." She gave me a fake grin and whipped around in her seat.

I looked over at Miss Sarah. I did not

like Lexie. I wondered if I could have a grown-up as a best friend. But would she want to be my friend? I was just temporary, like Lexie said.

Maybe this wouldn't be so fun after all. What was I going to do?

FAIRGROUND FACT #2

They call the circus the "big top" because at one time, circuses were always held in big tents. When the circus came to town, they would set up a tent in a big, open area. The workers put bleachers inside and everything. The tents were always really colorful, pretty, and huge.

Circuses mostly aren't in tents anymore. They're in big buildings like stadiums and arenas, where concerts and big ice-skating shows are held. This means instead of being in tents, animals like elephants and monkeys get to go inside those buildings. When the circus isn't going on, the animals stay outside in an area where they're safe.

CHAPTER
★ 3 ★

The bus was no fun. And we were on it for four whole hours. But the circus *was* funner!

Mom says "funner" isn't a word. It should be "more fun." "Funner" is a funner word, though.

"That's Lexie," I whispered to Miss Sarah as we watched her go into the aisle from her seat. "She doesn't like friends."

Miss Sarah told me it wasn't nice to talk

about people, but I didn't think it was nice to not be my best friend. I would have told Miss Sarah that, but we were rushing off the bus. And in front of us was a really big, fancy building.

We were in the middle of this town with buildings everywhere. The place where the circus was being held was called an "arena," and they had concerts and circuses and stuff there. Miss Sarah said so. She said they used to have these things in tents, but buildings were better because more people could fit in them.

The building was humongous. I looked up at it, my eyes wide. It was round like a spaceship, and there were lots of people going in and out of it.

And not just lots of people. There were also a lot of animals. Like elephants.

"ELEPHANTS!" a girl from the other bus screamed. She started running.

"April Capshaw," I heard a woman say. She was rushing after the girl, trying to catch up. She was saying the girl's full last name. That meant she should stop or else she was about to get in trouble. At least, that's what happened when my mom used my first and last name.

The girl didn't stop.

She probably would have run all the way to the elephant if a big guy hadn't picked her up. He lifted her way off the ground. I think that was almost as cool as petting an elephant. He had on overalls like Old MacDonald in the little play set I'd had when I was a kid. His belly was big like Santa's, and his head was completely bald. It was even shiny where the sun was hitting it.

"Whoa there, little missy," the big guy said cheerfully. "Where do you think you're going?"

And you know what? The girl kept running. Her legs were moving in the air like she was still running to the elephant.

The woman finally caught up with her. "April, get down from there."

"But—but—"

"I know, elephants," the woman said. "What did I tell you about elephants?"

The big guy let April down. She and the woman went inside.

"What did she tell her about elephants?" I asked Miss Sarah. 'Cause she should know.

"You can't play with them," Miss Sarah explained. "It's the rules."

"Ever?" Great. No friends and no elephants!

Miss Sarah laughed. "You can if you're supervised."

I wrinkled my nose, looking up at her. "Why?"

"Because those are the rules," Mom told us. "And we want to make sure you are safe."

I didn't know Mom was nearby. Was she spying on us? I started to get mad. But then I got an idea in my head. It just popped in there, from out of I-don't-know-where.

"Can Miss Sarah supervise me?" I said, excitement in my voice. "Please, please, please, please, please, please!"

One of my friends at my school said if you said "please" lots of times, sometimes moms said yes. Mostly they just said to stop saying "please," though.

"We have to get inside," Mom said.

I added more pleases. Lots of pleases. So many pleases, Mom made that face that said I'd gone too far.

She told me that sometimes. "Piper, you've gone too far." But I hadn't gone anywhere. Except a long, long way on a bus.

"Don't you want to see what inside looks like?" Mom asked.

Inside. I looked at the big building again. It was so pretty, with lots of windows. A big sign with the words THE CIRCUS COMES TO TOWN was hanging in front of it. It had lots of pretty colors.

"Yes!" I yelled. I tugged on Miss Sarah's hand.

"Piper," Mom said. "Be nice!"

I nodded at Mom and started pulling Miss Sarah toward the building. I could not wait to see all the stuff inside, and then I wanted to come back out to pet the elephants. Maybe they'd even let me feed them with peanuts. I'd seen that in a cartoon once.

Inside the building wasn't exciting at all. It was pretty boring. Just a big hallway with a bunch of people running around. A bunch of them were running the same way, though, so I tugged Miss Sarah's hand that way.

We followed two guys through a doorway that led into this big, huge room. A girl my age walked by holding a real-life monkey! I could do that.

"Can I do that?" I asked Miss Sarah. "I want to do that."

"Let's go meet Mr. Winkles," Mom said, still behind us.

Mr. Winkles. Was that the monkey? It sounded like a monkey's name.

Then I remembered Mr. Winkles was my mom's boss.

Mr. Winkles was standing near some guys who were putting up a small colorful wall on the floor. "That's a ring," Miss Sarah said. "There will be different rings around the floor."

I was still looking around when Mr. Winkles walked over to us. "You must be little Piper," he said, holding out his hand.

"I'm seven," I replied. Because seven isn't that little. I wanted to make that clear.

"Wow," he said, but I could tell he was just saying that.

"Piper likes animals," Miss Sarah said.

"I think we should make her a member of our Little Explorers Club."

"That sounds nice," Mom said.

"I'll tell you what," Mr. Winkles said. "Your mom and Sarah have work to do. While they're working, why don't I take you out and introduce you to Big Top Bubba?"

Big Top Bubba. I'd bet that was the elephant I saw outside. I started bouncing up and down on my heels. Finally! I couldn't wait to go.

"I'll be right in here if you need me," Mom said.

The elephants were outside. They'd have to come inside for the circus, though.

"How do the animals get in?" I asked Mr. Winkles as we walked. There were more people around now, and all of them seemed to walk faster when they saw Mr. Winkles.

Probably because he was the boss and they wanted him to think they were working hard.

"There are big doors at the back of the building," he said. "Sometimes they even drive cars in here. Wouldn't that be fun to see?"

Not really. I'd *much* rather see elephants walking around in there than cars driving around. But Mom said to always be nice to people, so I kept my lips tightly clamped together.

"Good afternoon," Mr. Winkles said to a man in overalls as we got closer to the place where all the animals were being kept. There was a big fence around the area.

The man Mr. Winkles was talking to was the one who had stopped that April girl from running earlier. He was a big guy, but he had a friendly face, so he wasn't scary-big.

"This is Piper," Mr. Winkles said. "She wants to be a Little Explorer."

I still wasn't sure what that was, but it had to be good. Especially since we were out here with the elephants.

"That's perfect!" the guy in overalls explained. "We just lost one of our explorers. She's a performer now."

"The girl with the monkey?" I asked Mr. Winkles.

"Yep," he said.

"I'm Big Top Bubba," the guy in overalls said.

Wait. Bubba was a *person*?

Bubba, who was not an elephant, shook my hand. He pointed to the elephant. "And this is Ella."

Ella the Elephant. I liked that.

"Would you like to take a ride with Ella?" Big Top Bubba asked. He grinned. "It's how we welcome new people here."

Would I? That would be the best thing ever!

I started bouncing up and down on my heels again.

I felt like I was on top of the world. I loved it.

Big Top Bubba walked with me the whole time, so it was safe. He was one of those people who can make animals behave. Not that he'd have to make Ella the Elephant behave. She was the best elephant ever.

Mom came out and watched for a while, but Mr. Winkles started talking to her and she left. I tried not to watch, but it looked like my mom might be in trouble. I hoped not. If she was in trouble, Mr. Winkles might make her leave, and then I wouldn't be able to play with the

elephants anymore. Or meet anyone new.

I wanted the circus to be my forever and ever home. I wanted to be a performer and have friends.

By the time we made it around the last time, I had an idea. It was the perfect plan.

"Can I work in the circus?" I asked Big Top Bubba as he started to walk to Ella's pen. "I could ride the elephant for everyone to see."

Big Top Bubba laughed. "Didn't anyone tell you?" he asked. "That's what a Little Explorer does. You'll be helping me."

That was the best news ever. It meant we could stay. I'd work really hard and be the best Little Explorer. That way they'd keep us around even if they got mad at my mom.

This was going to be way, *way* better than home. I could already tell.

FAIRGROUND FACT #3

Many circus performers actually start performing when they are children. The circus is a big family and circus kids train for years, imitating the grown-ups. When they aren't studying or playing, they're working hard, helping groom the animals and practicing things most kids would love to practice. Like walking a tightrope that's close to the ground.

In some circuses, children even get to ride the trapeze, which is a big swing that you can hang from with your legs or hands. You feel like you're flying!

CHAPTER
★ 4 ★

Being a Little Explorer was fun when I was the only one.

But I wasn't the only one.

There was that girl Big Top Bubba had stopped from running. Her name was April. She cried a lot. Plus a boy with funny hair named Davie. His brother, Chase, was afraid of clowns, which was bad since the circus had a lot of those! He kept hiding behind people whenever the clowns walked by.

Then there was Lexie. The girl who didn't like friends. She was a Little Explorer before I came, so she thought she was the boss of me. She thought she was the boss of everyone.

"You can't do that!" she yelled at me when I jumped in front of the line. We were practicing the dance Little Explorers always did during each show. I wanted to be in front. I was shortest, so it was only fair.

"Mr. Bubba!" April yelled. "Piper cut in line."

Did I mention April's a tattletale?

Big Top Bubba didn't want to get involved. He just shrugged and went back to wiping Ronnie, one of the elephants. I think Big Top Bubba is better with animals than people.

"You have to take turns," Davie said. "That's what my dad says."

"Your dad isn't in charge," Lexie pointed out. "Mr. Bubba is."

Lexie cut me in line, which meant she got to be in front. She also got to wear the hot pink costume when Miss Sarah surprised us with clothes for the show. I had to wear the light pink one.

Secretly, I liked the light pink one better, but I pretended to like the hot pink one because I knew Lexie would want it. I think April really liked the hot pink one too, because when Lexie took it, she cried.

Little Explorers had an important job to do. We had to do a fun dance that involved spinning around, waving our hands in the air, then kicking our feet up over and over again. Miss Sarah showed us how to kick gracefully and point our toes. After the dance was done, the pretty performers in sparkly costumes showed up. I was really nervous about it.

"You have to smile," Lexie told everyone when we were practicing the first day in our costumes. "And keep your head up high. No slouching!"

I made my smile as big as I could and looked at the other kids. They didn't look back. They must see lots of bossy Lexie.

"Thank you, Lexie," Miss Sarah said. "Now, why don't you show Piper where we change out of our costumes?"

Lexie frowned. But then she thought about it for a second and smiled. I knew what that meant. She was happy that she'd get to be the boss.

I had to run to keep up with Lexie,

who ran through two clowns practicing with a Hula-Hoop and a little sword, and jumped over a dog wearing a party hat. I wanted to stop to pet the dog, but I had to keep up.

There was a door with a paper sign taped to it. The words LITTLE EXPLORERS were written on the paper in black marker. It wasn't an official sign, but close.

"This is it," she said once we were inside. "Any questions?"

I knew if I said no, she'd run out. I didn't want her to run out. I wanted her to tell me circus stuff.

"Yes," I said. Then I thought and thought about what questions to ask. Looking around, I pointed at a long table. "What's that?"

Lexie looked where I was pointing.

"That's where we put on the makeup," she said.

I gasped. "We get to wear makeup?"

My mom would never, ever let me wear makeup. Makeup was for grown-ups, she said.

"Only because the lights make us look like we don't have it on at all," she said.

"Will you show me how to put makeup on?" I asked. "I don't know how."

She frowned at me. "The grown-ups will help us," she said. "Is that all?"

"No," I said."

I needed more questions. "Do you know the clowns?" I asked.

Lexie sighed. "That's a silly question."

"You don't know the clowns?" I asked. "Does April? Maybe April can introduce me."

Lexie's eyes got really wide then. "April doesn't know the clowns like I do. I know the clowns best."

And that's how I got Lexie to introduce me to the clowns.

FAIRGROUND FACT #4

Many circus performers are really very talented ballerinas and gymnasts who train for years. Some of them travel around, working for different circuses in between doing things like dancing in plays and ballets.

There's a college for circus performers, where you can take classes in dance, acting, and music. You can even go to college to become a clown. Some people say it's harder to get into the Ringling Bros. and Barnum & Bailey Clown College than Harvard Law School! Whether you go to school or not, you have to be really good to be a performer in a circus.

CHAPTER ★ 5 ★

Opening night was huge. Bigger than even the biggest elephant in the circus. I was so nervous, I could hardly stay in line. The mean woman with the clipboard and ear microphone thing kept pointing at me to tell me to get back in line.

Mom was nervous too. I noticed this morning that she'd been biting her nails again. She always bites her nails when she's stressed. I wanted to do the best job ever so she'd stop worrying and we could stay. No matter what she did, they wouldn't fire her if her daughter was the best Little Explorer ever in any circus anywhere.

I looked out in front of us. There was a big floor with lots of rings all around it. The audience was up in the bleachers above it. When we were practicing down there, the audience area was empty. Now that the seats were filled with people, all looking down at the floor where we'd be, it was *so* scary.

I was worrying so hard, I didn't even know it was time to go until Lexie started moving. That was when I stopped being scared that people would be staring at me and started being scared that I didn't remember the dance we'd practiced over and over and over.

"And now . . . welcome the Little Explorers!"

We all marched out, just like we'd practiced. I looked out at the crowd, squinting a little in the bright lights, waiting for our music to start.

Finally, the music began. Everyone started moving in time. Except me.

I didn't remember the dance.

I don't know where they went, but somehow the kicks and shuffles and pointed toes had escaped from my brain. All the steps I had practiced over and over were just . . . gone. I thought maybe I'd remember them once we kept on going.

Nope. Completely gone.

The best thing to do when you don't

know a dance is to look at the person next to you. The girls were in front and the boys were in back, so that person was April. April knew the dance. I'd just follow her.

There was just one problem with that. I was so busy trying to watch April, I started

to go off-balance. Before I could even stop, I bumpd into April!

"Oops, sorry!" I whispered. But it was too late.

April ended up crashing into Lexie. "Aaaah!" Lexie screeched as she fell back into the boys, who were now right in the path of the grown-ups who were coming in to start dancing behind us!

The whole dance was wrong for several minutes. By then the audience wasn't laughing or clapping. They were just quiet.

I'd messed the whole show up, just by looking at April and falling over. I'd messed all the dancers up, and now the dance was all wrong for everyone. I'd ruined the whole show. My mom would be in big, big trouble.

I knew that even before I saw Mr. Winkles, standing on the sidelines, staring at me with a big frown.

FAIRGROUND FACT #5

There are lots of superstitions in the circus, probably because people are walking on ropes so far above the ground. You need all the luck you can get when you're way up there. Here are a few circus superstitions:

#1 PERFORMERS ALWAYS ENTER THE RING WITH THEIR RIGHT FOOT FIRST.

#2 MANY CIRCUS PERFORMERS WON'T WEAR GREEN BECAUSE THEY THINK IT'S BAD LUCK.

#3 IF YOU SET YOUR SUITCASE DOWN BACKSTAGE, YOU AREN'T SUPPOSED TO MOVE IT AGAIN UNTIL YOU LEAVE FOR A NEW TOWN. (SERIOUSLY. HOW DO THEY GET THEIR CLOTHES OUT?)

CHAPTER
★ 6 ★

Mr. Winkles was not a happy camper. Not at all. He'd handed me over to Miss Sarah to "take care of the situation" and left.

"It'll be okay," she promised. "See? They are starting again already."

She pointed toward the door of the tiny dressing room where we were sitting. On the other side of it, we could hear applause. Then the music started up again.

"The show must go on," Miss Sarah explained. "That's what we say in the circus world when something happens."

I was probably supposed to smile at that, but I couldn't. All I could think was that Mr. Winkles was mad at me. And Mr. Winkles would fire my mom and not let me be a Little Explorer anymore. And we would have to leave.

"I have to go back out there," Miss Sarah said. "Why don't we go find your mom?"

I nodded. I wanted to know what was going on. If Mr. Winkles was yelling at her, I could say it's all my fault and he should yell at me instead.

So much for my plan to be the best Little Explorer ever. They could call me the *worst* Little Explorer ever. Lexie was probably the best.

When we got to the ring entrance, the show was almost over. Miss Sarah was biting her lip nervously. She wanted to perform, but she had to find my mom first.

"What are you doing back here?" one of the stage managers said when he saw us standing there, watching everything. "It's the big finale. Get out there."

Miss Sarah looked at me. I was expecting her to leave me with the stage manager, but she didn't. Instead, she grabbed my hand and pulled me out onto the floor.

I wanted to hide. I was sure when the audience saw me, they'd start booing. Instead, they started cheering louder. I didn't get it. I was the girl who had ruined the whole opening dance.

The other kids came out too, led by Lexie. She had this big smile on her face as she skipped over to stand next to me. She looked so beautiful—like a little fairy. I knew when people saw her, they had clapped for her instead of me.

After we finished bowing, we followed the performers back to all the dressing rooms. I stayed behind Lexie because she'd know where she was going. The other kids were with us. We all went back to the room where we'd been before the show. That was when I realized everyone was mad at me.

"The dance was all messed up," Lexie told me when I asked Davie what was wrong. "It's all your fault."

"I couldn't help it!" I said. Everyone shouldn't be mad at me. I was mad enough at me for all of us.

"You should just sit in the audience,"

Lexie said, shaking her head. "I don't think you should be a Little Explorer. I'm going to tell Mr. Bubba that."

I wanted to cry. If Mr. Bubba said I couldn't be a Little Explorer anymore, I'd be so sad. I wouldn't be able to even pet Ella anymore. Ella was the best friend I had here besides Miss Sarah.

Worst of all, if I was fired as a Little Explorer, they might fire my mom. That would mean I couldn't even *see* Ella anymore. I could see her if I went to the circus, but she'd be far away and I'd be in the audience.

That was why when Big Top Bubba walked by, I ran after him.

"I'm so, so, so sorry I made everyone fall," I said. "Please don't let me never see Ella again."

He'd been walking pretty fast, but when he heard me yelling after him, he turned to look at me and slowed down. "What?" he asked.

"I want to still be a Little Explorer," I said softly. Tears were rolling down my cheeks even though I didn't want them to be. Little Explorers were supposed to be strong.

He came back and knelt down in front of me. "Don't cry, little one," he said. "We

all make mistakes. Did you know one time
I lost an elephant?"

I wiped at my tears. "You can't lose an
elephant." I smiled. "They're too big."

"That's what I thought. But he wandered
away while we were loading the truck. This
big elephant was walking down the side-
walk in this city! People didn't know what

to think!" Bubba laughed a big belly laugh.

I laughed too. I was glad to be laughing instead of crying. "I'll bet people were surprised to see that."

"They were, but we found the elephant and everything was okay," he said. "Do you know what that means?"

I shook my head no.

"People make mistakes," he said. "Everyone does it. But it all worked out in the end and that's all that matters, right?"

I wasn't so sure.

"Come with me," Big Top Bubba said. "I want to show you something."

We walked back to the hallway where the clowns practiced. It was empty, but there were still props and costumes all around.

"Clowns mess up all the time," Big Top

Bubba said. "Once, Susie's Hula-Hoop went out into the audience in the middle of a show. Do you know what happened?"

I shook my head again.

"The other clowns jumped in and acted like it was all a part of the show." He gestured. "Come on."

We went to the area where the dogs were all running around. A trainer was trying to calm them down, but they were all over the place.

"Sometimes the dogs go all off track," Big Top Bubba said. "Denise here does the best she can, but when she needs help, do you know what she does? She signals and the other performers help."

"That's right," Denise said with a big smile.

"We all practice over and over, but

mistakes happen," Big Top Bubba said. "They happen all the time. When they do, we help each other out. That's what a family does."

"Family?" I asked, not sure what he meant. Were these his brothers and sisters?

"The circus is a family," he said. "And you're part of it now. Welcome to the family, Piper!"

I smiled. I liked the sound of that.

FAIRGROUND FACT #6

The circus has its own lingo. Here are a few words you'd know if you worked in the circus.

JOEY—ANOTHER WORD FOR A CLOWN. IF A GUY NAMED JOEY WAS A CLOWN, HE'D BE "JOEY THE JOEY."

ROUSTABOUT—SOMEONE WHO WORKS HARD GETTING THE RING READY FOR THE BIG NIGHT.

CANDY BUTCHERS—THE PEOPLE WHO SELL CANDY AND POPCORN AT THE CIRCUS. DON'T CALL THEM THAT TO THEIR FACES, THOUGH.

FIRST OF MAY—THAT'S WHAT THEY CALL NEW CIRCUS PERFORMERS. AS IN, "LOOK AT THAT FIRST OF MAY."

CHAPTER
★ 7 ★

Mom wanted to have a "special talk" about what happened last night. But it was while we were on the way to breakfast. In our circus, everyone had breakfast together every morning. Some of the kids sat together, but I didn't. I usually sat with the grown-ups.

"It can be scary being up in front of all those people," Mom said.

We'd been talking about the elephants

two seconds before, so it was confusing at first. I thought she meant the elephants.

"I know you got scared last night," Mom explained. "Don't feel bad about that. You just have to keep trying. It gets easier each time." She smiled at me and took my hand.

I looked over at my mom. Did she know? Had she been up in front of people before? She was really pretty and had a great singing voice. Maybe . . .

"Have you done it?" I asked. "Were you up in front of people once?"

"Only in school," Mom said. "Sometimes you have to get up and do speeches in front of your class."

I nodded. I had to do that once. I had to tell my class last year what I'd done during summer vacation. I was *so* scared. But I did it, and after people asked me all about our camping trip.

"Now that you've been up in front of a whole circus audience, it will be easier to do little things like that," Mom said. "Getting up in front of a class will seem like nothing."

We were in the big room with all the tables by then. That was where we always had breakfast. I didn't really want to sit with all those people, though. I wanted to have time with just my mom.

"You know what?" Mom said, like she was reading my mind. "I think we should sit over here. We should have breakfast together."

She pointed to a small table in the

corner. There was just room for two people. It was short, too, like it was made for kids. Mom gestured for me to follow, and we sat there together, me comfortable and Mom all squished to fit.

And that was when our daily mom-daughter breakfasts began.

FAIRGROUND FACT #7

Circus workers do everything together, including eating meals as a group. They become like one big happy family, watching out for one another's kids and doing assigned chores that keep everything running. Can you imagine traveling around the country with a bunch of kids your age and their parents? It would be like having all your sisters and brothers, cousins, and aunts and uncles in one big place.

CHAPTER
★ 8 ★

"**Does everyone have it down?**" Miss Sarah asked.

We'd been practicing the dance over and over again for so long, my feet hurt. But I couldn't complain. *I* was the reason we were doing all this.

"I do," Lexie said. "*I* always do."

I knew she meant that *I* didn't. I looked at the other Little Explorers. None of them was looking at me. They were all mad, I could tell. Davie even stuck his tongue out at me when Miss Sarah wasn't looking.

One by one, the Little Explorers left for lunch. I stayed at the back of the line, walking slowly. I didn't want to be near the other Little Explorers.

When we passed Big Top Bubba in the hallway, he stopped. He put a hand on each hip and looked down at me.

"Why aren't you walking with them?"

"They don't like me anymore," I said.

He made a frowny face. Then he followed the line of Little Explorers toward the eating room.

I sped up my steps then. I had to catch up with everyone to see what Big Top Bubba would do.

They weren't even in the eating room. They were standing outside, all gathered in a group, with Big Top Bubba kneeling down in front of them.

"She messes everything up," Lexie said.

"Everyone makes mistakes," Big Top Bubba told all of them.

"Can we go now?" Chase asked.

"What if one of you makes a mistake tonight?" Big Top Bubba asked. "What if everyone gets mad at you and won't forget about it? How would that make you feel?"

Everyone got all squirmy. Even Lexie. She looked over at me.

"I'm trying my best," I said.

"Maybe you can help," Big Top Bubba said to Lexie. "You're an expert. Why don't you be Piper's mentor?"

"What's that?" Chase asked, wrinkling up his nose.

"A mentor is someone who teaches you

things," Big Top Bubba explained. "Lexie knows a lot about working in the circus, right?"

All the Little Explorers nodded. Lexie didn't.

"Then, Lexie, it's your job to help Piper," he continued. "You're her number one buddy. Her mentor. Be good to her."

Big Top Bubba stood up, and everyone else ran into the room where the food was. Lexie came over to where I was standing. "Come on," she said. "We need to eat. We're going to practice the dance until you're the best circus performer ever."

I smiled, but only after Lexie turned her back. I didn't want her to know I'd seen that she was excited to be helping me. Maybe Lexie wasn't so mean after all.

FAIRGROUND FACT #8

Elephants are the biggest land animals in the world, with some as tall as nine feet high! They can live seventy years, almost as long as most humans. Without circuses and zoos, you'd have to go somewhere like Africa or Asia to see a real-life elephant.

Most elephants you see in the circus are female, since male elephants can sometimes become aggressive. The most famous elephant ever was Jumbo, an elephant that was twelve feet high. People all over the world loved Jumbo. There's even a statue of him in Canada. He was so popular, he gave us the word "jumbo," which we still say today.

CHAPTER
★ 9 ★

It was the best surprise ever.

Miss Sarah put me in a pretty pink dress and put sparkles around my eyes. She even curled my hair. The dress had a puffy skirt so I had to keep pushing it down, but I loved it. I looked like a real-life circus performer.

While she was fixing my hair, we talked about the other Little Explorers.

"Lexie can be a little . . . princessy,"

Miss Sarah said. "She's been a Little Explorer since she was only three."

I gasped. Three years old! That was young. I wish I could have been in the circus when I was only three.

"But you're lucky to have her to help," Miss Sarah said with a wink. "She's really smart about this stuff."

Lexie came and got me once I was dressed. She wanted to do the dance one more time in our dresses. She thought that would make us better. We were on our third time through when Miss Sarah came and got us.

"It's showtime," she said with a big smile.

As we waited in line at the curtain, I expected Lexie to tell me not to mess this up. Instead, she turned around and said words that made me feel happy.

"You can do this," she declared. "Give me your hand."

I held up my hand, not sure what she was going to do. She grabbed it like a handshake, then pulled it back toward her. She then lifted her hand above mine like she wanted to do a low five. It was a secret handshake!

I'd never been part of a secret handshake before. This was super cool. We went through the steps and smiled at each other.

"For luck," she said. Then she turned to face front again.

I took a deep breath. This was it. I'd messed up the last time, but they'd let me try again. I had to show everyone that I could be a good circus performer. I could dance and smile and not forget my steps.

We walked to our spot and stopped. We

were supposed to wait until the announcer told everyone we were the Little Explorers. April didn't wait.

She just started dancing.

I wanted to wait, but next thing I knew, everyone around me was dancing. So I started dancing too. Only we were *all* completely off this time on what we were supposed to do and we were all ruining the show. All of us together. Well, actually, not together at all.

It was such a mess, there didn't seem to be a way to fix it. I thought about yelling out that everyone should stop and start over. Miss Sarah was standing on the sidelines, a hand on each side of her face. She seemed to be frozen.

I had to do something. I had to do something to save the show. Maybe I could do a trick. I knew how to do a cartwheel.

The audience would see my cartwheel and cheer. I knew they would. So I waited until everyone was busy doing other things, chose a space, and did a cartwheel. When that went well, I did another and another. I was glad I had kept my shorts on under my dress.

The end of my fifth cartwheel was when things got bad. That was when I stood up and realized I was right in the path of a clown balancing on a ball. His big smile changed to an *O* shape and he started trying to get his footing right. He went to the left—right into the animal trainer who was controlling a line of dogs.

Dogs went in every direction, barking and yipping. Some ran toward where Miss Sarah was, others went toward the audience, and others went to the backstage area.

All I could think was: I'd ruined the circus *again*.

Nobody would ever forgive me this time.

FAIRGROUND FACT #9

Sometimes clowns do a trick called "clown car," where a bunch of clowns squeeze into a car and come out, one by one. People think it has to be a trick, but it isn't. They take out as much of the inside of the car as they can, even the seats. This makes lots of room so clowns can squeeze in.

Usually fifteen to twenty clowns can squeeze into one of those small cars. But it isn't just the clowns. If you go to a circus with a clown car, you'll see they have suitcases, beach balls, and other items to make it funnier. All of that fits into one little car!

I guess each clown holds his breath until it's time to get out.

CHAPTER ★10★

I could fix this. I *would* fix this.

I had to fix this. If I didn't, we'd be fired for sure. No more wearing fancy ballerina clothes. No more Ella the Elephant. And I'd *never* have any friends.

Everyone would be mad at me now. Not just Lexie and the other Little Explorers. The whole audience, the performers, Big Top Bubba. . . . That made me very, very sad.

Dogs were barking and people in the

audience were being really, really noisy, but I paid no attention to that. I ran after the line of dogs and began trying to round them up.

"Come on, guys," I said. "This way!"

At first I thought I might be making them mad by forcing them to go somewhere without knowing where they were going. But then I got one into the ring and went after another. Soon three were in the ring and I was all excited.

Then one jumped back out.

I chased after it, running around in circles, shouting. I got one back in and found out the other two had escaped. Dogs were everywhere and soon monkeys were too. It was the worst circus ever!

That was when I heard something weird.

The audience was laughing.

At me.

I should stop now. I was only making it worse. My mom would be so disappointed that I'd gotten her fired, and they were laughing at me. For the rest of forever, people would talk about the girl who had ruined the circus not once, but twice.

I came to a stop and looked for a way to escape. There were lots of exits, but none of them was close by. I could run, but everyone would be watching.

Then something bad happened. Something worse than laughing.

Silence.

Silence was worse than laughing, I decided. Silence didn't happen in the circus. Ever. As I looked for a place to exit, I saw my mom. She looked worried. She knew we would be fired now.

I turned around and looked at the other performers. They were smiling, not laughing. Miss Sarah moved up in front of all of it and started clapping really high in the air. That was when something magical happened.

The audience started clapping too.

Someone whistled, and someone else yelled, "Go! Go! Go! Go! Go!"

"Everyone, let's hear it for Piper Morgan!" the guy with the microphone said.

They weren't laughing at me. They wanted me to fix this. The show must go on, as Miss Sarah said!

I could do it. So I went. I kept chasing dogs even though I'd never ever catch them. I tried to be as funny as I could too. I hunched over a little and reached my arms straight out in front of me and ran, ran, ran.

Dogs were really hard to catch. But I had an idea.

"Lexie! Help me!" I yelled. At first she looked a little surprised that I was asking her to do something. Then she started laughing and running with me. Soon all the Little Explorers were running around, trying to catch the dogs.

The audience exploded into applause. I stopped chasing dogs and looked up at them all. I didn't know what to do.

"Bow," Miss Sarah whispered.

So I bowed. And the audience clapped and cheered! Lexie ran over and bowed next to me. The other Little Explorers, all wanting to do their parts of the show, ran over to us.

Miss Sarah took us all backstage. They were moving on to the trapeze artists until they could get the dogs all gathered up, Miss Sarah said. I'd done it! I'd saved the show—the show was going on, just as Miss Sarah had said it would.

"Wasn't that the most fun ever?" I asked Lexie.

Lexie got a pouty face for a second, and

I thought maybe she was mad. Instead, she changed her pouty face into a smile.

"Yes," she agreed. "*Ever,* ever."

A couple of weeks later my mom gave me a big surprise. It wasn't the good kind of surprise either.

We were eating breakfast in our RV when she said it. Our RV had become so much like our real home had been. Mom decorated it with all our favorite things, including the big stuffed bear that had been my favorite when I was little.

The other RVs were nice, but not like mine. I even had my own little room. It was the living room during the day, but at night it became my room with my favorite fluffy blanket and a night-light in case I got scared.

"You're going back to school," she said while we were eating breakfast. She wanted to have breakfast in the RV, sitting on top of the bed when it was made up. We never did that.

"I know!" I said. I smiled even bigger. "Miss Sarah said I get a tutor."

Mom got that look. You know the look. It's the one grown-ups get when they have to tell you something you don't want to hear.

"I told you this job was just temporary," she said in the nice voice she uses when she is telling me bad news. "This came up quicker than I expected."

"But you said it could become something longer," I said. "I like the circus."

"This is going to be a new adventure," Mom said. "You may even like it better."

I wasn't smiling anymore.

"I know you really liked being here—," Mom started to say.

"I have friends here," I interrupted. I knew it was not nice to interrupt, but this was important. Life or death almost. "And the elephants like me."

"There will be new friends," Mom said quietly.

"Not like these," I said. "And I've been doing a really good job. I'm getting along with Lexie and everything."

"I know, and I'm really proud of you," Mom said. "I'm sure you'll do a really good job helping me at the school, too."

I frowned. All my hard work and we were still leaving? It wasn't fair.

"There aren't elephants in schools," I told her, hoping that would help.

"It's a nice school, though," Mom said.

"I'm going to be helping out in the principal's office."

I thought about that for a second. I didn't like the principal's office. It was a scary place. But if my mom worked there, I might get to sit behind the principal's desk and play on the computers like I worked there.

But there was something even better about going back to school.

"We're going home!" I said. I started jumping up and down. This was the bestest news ever.

"No, Piper, we're not. We're still going to live with Nanna. But it's a new adventure."

I did want to see Nanna.

"Plus, we may be able to stay there," Mom said. "We just have to do a really good job and impress them, and maybe that will be our new home. We could find our own apartment."

Permanent! Yay!

Then I remembered something, and my smile turned into a frown.

"But what about Ella?" I asked. "And Big Top Bubba? And Lexie? And . . . and . . . Miss Sarah!"

The circus was going to a place called Missouri next. I'd never been to Missouri, but I'd seen it on the map in my classroom when I was in school. I wanted to go to Missouri so I could point to it on a map and say I'd been there.

Mom wasn't listening to me at all. She was putting our clothes in our suitcases. She just wanted to get out of there. I knew what I had to do.

I ran as fast as my feet would carry me.

I ran even though my mom was yelling for me. I ran even though people had to jump out of the way to keep me from knocking into them. I ran and ran and ran until I found Lexie.

She was with Miss Sarah and the Little Explorers and a bunch of performers. They were watching the animal trainers as they loaded animals into trucks. I wanted to watch the elephant trainers. But we had to go.

"We're going to my nanna's house," I said. I was moving back and forth like I was doing a new Little Explorer's dance.

"You are?" Lexie asked. She sounded sad. "But I was going to invite you to a sleepover. Just us. It was going to be fun. And what about the performance? We had a lucky secret handshake and everything."

I'd been right all along. Lexie was my friend. And it was the best kind of best friend ever because she was going to be a real-life circus performer when she grew up.

"I liked being your friend, Lexie," I said. "You were a good friend. But we have to go."

"We're going to miss you," Miss Sarah said, kneeling down so she was at my level.

"We don't want you to go," Chase said. "You made the circus fun."

"You did," Miss Sarah said. She looked over at the Little Explorers. "But Piper will visit us sometime, right?"

"Piper!" my mom yelled. "Come back here! We're leaving soon!"

I looked at Lexie. "Maybe we can keep in touch?" I asked.

"Cool," Lexie said. At least she'd said something besides "bye."

"You'll be here forever," I told Lexie.

I put my hand over my heart just like my mom showed me the last time I said bye to my friend.

Lexie looked weird for a second, then smiled. "Have fun at your nanna's," she said. "Maybe when you grow up, you can come back and we can be performers together."

I liked the sound of that. Being in the circus had to be the best job ever. I'd never find one better, I was sure of it.

A taxi was coming to take Mom and me to a place where we could rent a car. While we were waiting, we talked about what a best friend was.

But you know what I was thinking? I

was thinking that maybe sometimes it's fun to meet new people. Maybe permanent wasn't so good after all. I'd met a ballerina and an elephant and got to be a star because things weren't permanent.

I couldn't wait to see what happened next.

ACKNOWLEDGMENTS

Thank you to my incredible editor, Alyson Heller; awesome illustrator, Lucy Fleming; and everyone on the editing, publicity, and design team at Simon & Schuster. You're changing the world one book at a time. Also thank you to my supportive, talented, amazing agent, Natalie Lakosil. You all make me a better writer.

I also need to mention the writers in my online community who support me in everything I do. Here they are in alphabetical order: Alex J. Cavanaugh, Beth Ellyn Summer, Beverly Stowe McClure, Cathrina Constantine, Elizabeth Seckman, Jessica Haight, Kelly Hashway, Kristin Smith, Leandra J. Wallace, Medeia Sharif, Meradeth Houston, Sandra Cox, S. K. Anthony,

Stephanie Robinson, and T. B. Markinson. You guys are the best.

And lastly, my family, who are always there for me, cheering me on. Neil and Cambryn, Valerie and Doug, Marquita and John, Jennifer and Seth, and Hollis and Rhett. Without you, Piper wouldn't even exist because I wouldn't have been able to create her.

Don't miss Piper Morgan's
next adventure:

PIPER MORGAN IN CHARGE!

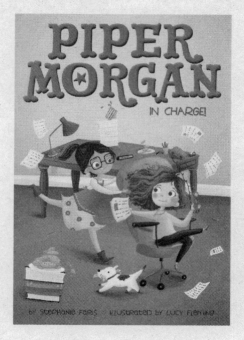